INTERNET ANIMAL STARS

CATS, CATS, CATS!

REBECCA FELIX

Lerner Publications ◆ Minneapolis

Lerner Publications Company
An imprint of Lerner Publishing Group, Inc.
241 First Avenue North
Minneapolis, MN 55401 USA

For reading levels and more information, look up this title at www.lernerbooks.com.
Main body text set in Caecilia Com
Typeface provided by Monotype

Library of Congress Cataloging-in-Publication Data

Names: Felix, Rebecca, 1984– author.
Title: Cats, cats, cats! / Rebecca Felix.
Description: Minneapolis : Lerner Publications, [2021] | Series: Internet animal stars | Includes bibliographical references and index. | Audience: Ages 6–10 | Audience: Grades 2–3 | Summary: "This guide educates young readers about the owners of the internet, the cat! Curricular content about the life cycle and habitat of domestic cats is paired with a fun, social-media-inspired design"— Provided by publisher.
Identifiers: LCCN 2019051187 (print) | LCCN 2019051188 (ebook) | ISBN 9781541597136 (library binding) | ISBN 9781728402871 (paperback) | ISBN 9781728400358 (ebook)
Subjects: LCSH: Cats—Juvenile literature.
Classification: LCC SF445.7 .F45 2021 (print) | LCC SF445.7 (ebook) | DDC 636.8—dc23

LC record available at https://lccn.loc.gov/2019051187
LC ebook record available at https://lccn.loc.gov/2019051188

Manufactured in the United States of America
1 – CG – 7/15/20

PAGE PLUS

Scan QR codes throughout the book for videos of cute animals!

Introduction

CATS, CATS, CATS!

What do you know about cats? These furry animals are the smallest members of the feline family. Cats are domestic. They live with and around humans. Cats also entertain humans! The internet is bursting with cute cat **content.** Dig your claws into cat facts. Then learn how cats became online sensations!

#FamilyFact

Lions and tigers are part of the feline family too.

Ameowzing!

Chapter 1

THAT CAT LIFE

Itty-Bitty Kitties

Baby cats are tiny! A newborn kitten is about as big and heavy as a deck of cards.

Newborn kittens sleep often. After two weeks, they are strong enough to stand. Then kittens begin to walk, **pounce**, and play.

ZZZZZZZZzz
Scan this QR code to see a playful kitten!

Aging Adults

After two to three months, kittens are old enough to be adopted as pets. They continue to grow and play.

Many kittens have tons of energy!

Cats age more quickly than humans. In only one year, cats reach adulthood. After age two, a cat ages four years for every human year.

#Cathlete

Seniors

Cat adulthood lasts about eight to ten years. After that, cats are seniors.

From kitten to senior, some cats stay **energetic.** Others snooze and lounge. Many cats are also **curious.**

Cat personalities **vary.** But all cats share the same basic needs.

Even old kitties pounce and play!

#CatNap

On average, cats sleep fifteen hours a day.

Scan this QR code to see a sleepy kitty!

Chapter 2

HOME BASE & STUFFING FACE

Cats can live indoors or outdoors. They are kept as pets in **climates** worldwide. Wherever cats live, it's in their nature to explore.

Provide pet cats with tall structures to scale. And give them cubbies to squish into!

#PurrfectFit

Cat-friendly homes also have special surfaces for scratching. Cats scratch to sharpen their claws and mark their **territories**.

#FurRealFact

Cats can't taste sweet things.

Cats use their claws to hunt. Cats hunt birds, mice, and other small animals. But most pet cats eat prepared food. This food can be dry or wet.

Cat food is often meat flavored.

Cats that eat prepared food still have the **instinct** to hunt. Give pet cats toys to bat around, pounce on, and chase!

Whether through toys, snacks, or snuggles, cats need attention. Happy cats capture the world's attention.

So do grumpy cats,
doofy cats,
and floofy cats!

Chapter 3

CATS IN POP CULTURE

Today, cats are internet royalty! But how and why did these purring pets become **beloved** online?

Researchers say felines' rise to internet fame began in 2007. That year, a website called I Can Haz Cheezburger made cat memes popular. Soon, cat content filled the internet.

Experts think cat behaviors made the animals online stars. Cat reactions can be **unpredictable**. This can lead to funny content.

Cat pounces, stares, and naps are also adored online. And many people just think cats are cute!

Several cute and kooky cats have become social media celebrities.

#Caticorn

★ Celeb Kitties ★

Internet cat stars become famous for many reasons. Some star in a single meme. Others have their own social media accounts, websites, and more!

Superstar! GRUMPY CAT

Grumpy Cat lived from 2012 to 2019. Feline **dwarfism** made her face look grumpy. Grumpy Cat appeared in many memes, gifs, and videos. Companies also made Grumpy Cat books and toys.

MEME BREAK!

WHEN YOUR TEACHER ASKS YOU FOR THE ANSWER, BUT YOU'VE BEEN DAYDREAMING FOR THE LAST TEN MINUTES

WHEN YOUR PARENTS GIVE YOU TEN CHORES
ON TOP OF THE THIRTY CHORES YOU ALREADY HAVE

WHEN MOM WALKS IN AND ASKS HOW YOU AND YOUR LITTLE BROTHER ARE GETTING ALONG

CHATTING WITH YOUR BESTIE AFTER SCHOOL
TO TALK ABOUT WHAT YOU DID IN SCHOOL
EVEN THOUGH YOU SAW EACH OTHER
ALL DAY AT SCHOOL

MEME BREAK!

Conclusion

CATS ROCK!

Cat stars have staying power! Cat content has remained popular for years.

These cats also make a positive **impact.** Their popularity encourages pet adoption. And it **inspires** people to accept disabilities and unique looks.

People celebrate internet cats at festivals and by buying **merchandise**.

Many cat celebs have made their owners into millionaires.

beloved: loved very much

climate: the usual weather patterns of a place

content: ideas, facts, and images available online

curious: wanting to know more about something

dwarfism: a condition that causes people and animals to stop growing when they are small

energetic: having a lot of energy

impact: to affect something

inspire: to cause someone to want to do something

instinct: a natural behavior or feeling that is not learned

merchandise: things that are bought and sold

pounce: to suddenly jump onto something

territory: an area that an animal uses and protects

unpredictable: behaving in a way that is unexpected

vary: to be different

WEBSITES

Animal Planet—Cats 101
https://www.animalplanet.com/tv-shows/cats-101/videos/all-about-kittens
Learn about different cat breeds in short, funny, informative videos.

Ducksters—Cats
https://www.ducksters.com/animals/cats.php
Read about cat behavior, breeds, and more. Then learn fun and silly cat facts!

National Geographic Kids—Cats Quiz Whiz
https://kids.nationalgeographic.com/games/quizzes/cats-quiz-whiz/
Test your cat-fact knowledge by taking a cat-themed quiz.

BOOKS

Drimmer, Stephanie Warren. *Cat Breed Guide: A Complete Reference to Your Purr-fect Best Friend*. Washington, DC: National Geographic, 2019.
Learn more about cat breeds and discover how to choose the right one as a pet. Read about cats in history and pop culture.

Miller, Kelley. *Just Joking: Cats*. Washington, DC: National Geographic, 2016.
Discover fantastic feline jokes and silly kitty photos. Then read about famous cat stars of the internet!

Rober, Harold T. *I Love Cats*. Minneapolis: Lerner Publications, 2017.
Learn more about keeping cats as pets. Read about cat behaviors and supplies!